THIS BRAVE BUNNIES BOOK
BELONGS TO

BRAVE BUNNIES™

glowberry

LADYBIRD BOOKS

UK | USA | Canada | Ireland | Australia | India | New Zealand | South Africa

Ladybird Books is part of the Penguin Random House group of companies
whose addresses can be found at global.penguinrandomhouse.com.

www.penguin.co.uk   www.puffin.co.uk   www.ladybird.co.uk

Penguin
Random House
UK

First published 2022
001

This book is based on the TV series *Brave Bunnies*
Text and illustrations © 2022 GLOWBERRY BOOKS PUBLISHING HOUSE LTD;
© 2022 ANIMA KITCHENT MEDIA S.L.
Adapted by Rachel Elliot

Brave Bunnies is created by Olga Cherepanova and Anna Sarvira.
© 2022 GLOWBERRY BOOKS PUBLISHING HOUSE LTD;
© 2022 ANIMA KITCHENT MEDIA S.L. All Rights Reserved.

Printed in China

The authorized representative in the EEA is Penguin Random House Ireland,
Morrison Chambers, 32 Nassau Street, Dublin D02 YH68

A CIP catalogue record for this book is available from the British Library

ISBN: 978-0-241-49019-8

All correspondence to:
Ladybird Books, Penguin Random House Children's
One Embassy Gardens, 8 Viaduct Gardens, London SW11 7BW

BRAVE BUNNIES™

SPRING TO THE RESCUE

Bop   Boo   Franny

It was a blustery day on the plains. The Brave Bunnies had set up their bunny-camp next to a little wood.

WHOOO! The whistling wind flapped the carrot-flag.

WHEEE! It gusted and blew.

"Look at me!" Boo giggled.
"My ears are flapping!"

SWOOSH!

The wind snatched the hat from Ma's head!

"We can help you look for your hat, Ma!" said Bop.

"Yes!" said Boo. "We're good finders!"
Bop and Boo dashed into the wood.

Ma followed them with the babies.
"I'll check behind these ferns," said Ma.

"We'll look over there,"
said Bop, feeling excited.
This was a real quest!

Bop and Boo were running past a wildflower patch when they heard a loud voice.

A little fox holding a wand and a shield
leaped out in front of them.

"I'm Franny the Fearless Fox!" said the fox.
Bop and Boo shared a bunny-smile. Hooray!
Time to make a new friend!

"I'm Bop, the **BRAVE BUNNY!**" said Bop.

"I'm Boo. I'm a **BRAVE BUNNY!**, too," said Boo.

Boo gazed at Franny.
"I like your wand and shield," said Boo.
"Thanks!" said Franny in a bold voice.
"I'm a hero looking for **adventure!**"

"We have the perfect one!" said Bop.
"Will you help us search for Ma's hat?"

"Queen Bunny has lost her crown?" said Franny.
"Never fear! We three brave heroes will find it!"
She held up her wand and looked at Bop and Boo.
They needed wands, too!

Bop found two PERFECT sticks on the ground.

"We must search high and low for Ma's hat!" said Bop.

The wind made strange noises
as it whistled through the trees.

HOWWWL!
WHOOSH!

"What was that?" Boo asked.
There was only one way to find out!

DUH-DUH-DA-DUH!

Fearless Franny charged off to explore,
with the Brave Bunnies close behind her.
"Come on, Queen Bunny!" Boo called to Ma.

The adventurers bounded through the wood.

They leaped over ferns . . .

and weaved between birch trees.

At last, they reached a clearing with an old gnarled tree in the centre. Its branches waved and whirled in the wild wind.

HOWWWL!

"The sound's coming from that tree!" Bop exclaimed.

"That's not a tree!" Franny gasped.

"It's a HUGE HOWLING GIANT!"

Bop and Boo stared up
at the tree-giant.

Its long whirling branches were like
arms trying to grab them.

"Is it a mean giant?"
Boo asked in a small voice.

"The meanest!" said Franny, smiling at Boo.
"But we're not scared, right, Brave Boo?"

"Right, Fearless Franny!" said Boo.

"Look! The giant took Ma's hat!"
Bop shouted. The hat was sticking
out from a big hollow in the
trunk of the tree-giant.

"It's got it in its
great-big hungry
mouth," said Bop.
"What if it eats it?"
Boo cried.

Fearless Franny looked up
at Ma and smiled.

"Don't worry, Your Majesty," Franny said.
"We'll rescue your crown!"

WHOOSH! HOWWWL!

The wind blew wildly, and the tree-giant's branches whirled and waved.

"Crunching carrots!" Bop yelled.
"Watch out for its long grabby arms!"

DUH-DUH-DA-DUH!

Franny and Bop charged towards the tree-giant, but Boo held back. She thought it looked scary!

Bop hopped and hopped, but it was no use. He wasn't tall enough.

"I can't reach the crown!" he said. "Help, Brave Boo."

"You're the only one who can save it!" said Franny.

Boo felt scared, but she knew
that her friends needed her.

DUH-DUH-DA-DUH!

BRAVE
BUNNY,
AWAY!

Franny lent Boo
her wand, and Bop
gave her a
bunny-boost-up.
Boo reached . . .
and stretched . . .

and knocked the crown out of
the tree-giant's mouth-hollow.

"Got it!" Boo cheered.

"Boo, you've saved Queen Bunny's crown," said Franny.

"You're a true Brave Bunny hero!"

"HOORAY!"

WHOOO!
WHEEE!
HOWWWL!

The tree-giant bent and swayed. Its branch-arms waved wildly. "Quick, before the giant tries to steal it back!" cried Franny.

Giggling, Bop, Boo and
Franny ran to Ma.

"Here's your crown, Queen Bunny," said Boo.
"Thank you, brave heroes," said Ma, smiling.

While Queen Bunny put on her crown,
the three brave heroes sang a song.

"We're best friends!
Best bunny-friends!

"We did it!"